Quran Stories for Little Believers

CW00327736

The Spider's House

by

SANIYASNAIN KHAN

Goodword kidz

Helping you build a family of faith

2

Have you
ever seen the
spider's little
house—the
cobweb?

Have you
ever thought how
the spider spins
its web?

4

6

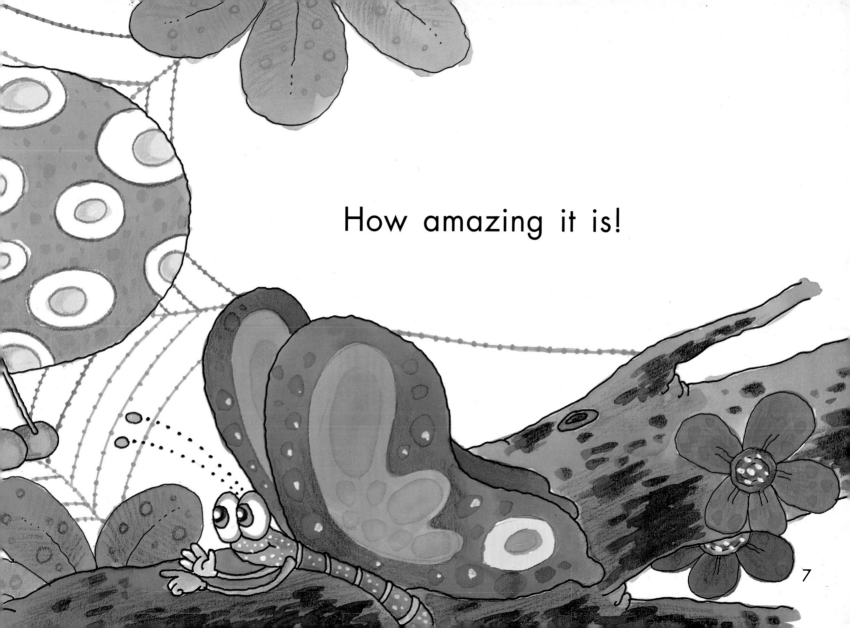

How amazing it is!

7

8

The thread of the spider's
web is stronger than steel
of the same thickness.

9

The thread of the spider's web can be stretched to four times its length.

But still the spider's house is the weakest of all the houses.